MW01174697

Healthy Mom Healthy Me

Helping Kids When Mom's Sick

Gwen Ratermann

Balboa Press books may be ordered through booksellers or by contacting:

Balboa Press
A Division of Hay House
1663 Liberty Drive
Bloomington, IN 47403
www.balboapress.com
1 (877) 407-4847

Because of the dynamic nature of the Internet, any web addresses or links contained in this book may have changed since publication and may no longer be valid. The views expressed in this work are solely those of the author and do not necessarily reflect the views of the publisher, and the publisher hereby disclaims any responsibility for them.

Any people depicted in stock imagery provided by Thinkstock are models, and such images are being used for illustrative purposes only. Certain stock imagery © Thinkstock.

ISBN: 978-1-4525-9033-2 (sc)
ISBN: 978-1-4525-9034-9 (e)

Library of Congress Control Number: 2014900547

Printed in the United States of America.

Balboa Press rev. date: 01/15/2014

BALBOA.
PRESS
A DIVISION OF HAY HOUSE

Healthy Mom Healthy Me

Table of Contents

For all the children and their families whose lives have been impacted by illness, that they may find health and mental well-being.

Acknowledgements

I am incredibly grateful to all of the family and friends throughout my life that encouraged me to pursue my writing craft.

Healthy Mom Healthy Me is my second book and has been shepherded along by a number of wonderful people. My friend, Joan Kelly, encouraged me to write the first chapter for children of a good friend of hers who had been diagnosed with a brain tumor. That first foray into writing for children became the impetus for this book.

My first and most important editor is young Elsa Kelley-Marcum. She read the first chapter and then when I finished the whole book, she was kind enough to give me her additional feedback. Her mom, Christina Kelley, encouraged me as well – her encouragement was the nudge I needed to write the full text.

Since I was new at writing for this age group, it was crucial for me to find an editor who worked with first and second graders to keep me on target for their reading needs. My husband's cousin, Jane McCarthy, was the perfect person for this job. She was a school teacher for 30 years and her input on the content and look of the text was important. I sure appreciate Jane's valuable time and expertise in making the book as accessible as possible to my young readers.

I must thank Brian Beahan, my son-in-law, for his advice on publishers and leading me to my illustrator, Wendy Leach. My thanks to Wendy as well; her sweet illustrations have brought the text to life. I also appreciate all the help I received from the folks at Balboa Press. They are great crew to work with.

Finally, my heartfelt thanks goes to my husband, Martin, and daughters, Sarah and Beth. Martin endured the horrors of cancer and survived, and we learned these coping lessons together during that challenging time in our lives. I am grateful to be here on the other side of that life chapter to share what we have learned with others.

An Introduction for You and Your Mom

My dear friend, Joan, messaged me on Facebook a few months ago and said a good friend of hers was recently told she had a brain tumor. This young woman is in the prime of her life with a successful career as a healthcare CEO and two small children.

Joan remembered that I drew a simple picture of my husband, Marty, when he was ill with stage VI cancer that helped me, our girls, family and friends to focus on his good health. It was a large stick figure filled with yellow crayon, outlined in blue, a big red heart on the chest and a huge smile beaming on his face.

I had written a blog about how I started drawing the figures, one after another, to help me to rise above my sheer panic and sadness. I drew the figures with crayon, one right after another, and taped them up all over my work office. I used up the bright yellow crayon in one box and had to raid other crayon boxes for that particular color --- yellow, the color of light and health.

In the blog I described how my co-workers started posting my drawings in their offices, our family and friends started posting them on their refrigerators at home or at their desk at work. I started calling the picture "Healthy Marty".

Working for a printer at the time, our daughter, Beth, had 50 copies made of the picture and sent to our home so we could display them everywhere. One Sunday our oldest daughter Sarah and I posted them on Marty's workshop, on his bike, on the clothes line, even on the back of the shorts he was wearing – trying to celebrate our belief in his health.

Marty has survived and I shared this blog and the picture with many others. I drew a healthy girl picture when a female family member was diagnosed with colon cancer. I sent her the "Healthy Marty" story and months later she shared that the simple picture and visualization of health helped her.

So the sharing continues. Joan asked me to write the story for her friend's children, and I did. I asked a friend if her eight-year-old would edit the story for me and Elsa did not change a word. Afterwards, her mother encouraged me to write a book, and here we are.

I am including not only the "Healthy Marty" story and visualization – which I have now changed to "Healthy Mom", but a few other simple tools children and adults can use to help them to navigate the incredibly stressful and emotionally ravaging throes of dealing with a parent with a serious illness.

The other sections of this book describe how developing an attitude of gratitude can lift our spirits, keeping a journal can be a very special personal counselor and expressing our anger or other feelings is a very important thing to do.

These simple tools have helped me and my family. I hope they can help you too.

Healthy Mom

Your mom is one of the very most important people in your world. When she gets sick, you feel really sorry for her and you want to do something to help her to feel better. Sometimes, if she is really feeling bad, you feel scared too. You want her to feel better so she can be back to her very special self and your family can be happy and back to normal again.

This is a simple picture that you can use to help you to keep your mom's good health and happiness in your minds and hearts. Looking at it can remind you that she will be back to her normal self before long, and this is a constant reminder of her being happy and healthy again.

This picture is simple so it can be for any mom, and it is yellow because yellow is the color of light and reminds many people of goodness and health. This yellow woman has a big red heart because every mom has the biggest heart we can imagine.

You can make copies of this picture and put them where ever you are – on the kitchen refrigerator, in your bedroom, stuck in a book you have at school – anywhere you are where you need to be reminded to think happy thoughts about your mom getting better. And the pictures can help you to remember to say a little prayer for her, for you and for your family as you help each other to be strong.

You can also make your own picture of your mom being happy and healthy – and put copies of it everywhere you look. You can make your picture look like her, because you know better than anyone how beautiful she is. Share these pictures with your family and friends so they can help in thinking about your mom's health and happiness.

Healthy Mom pictures for you

1. How does this Healthy Mom picture make you feel?

   I am feeling

2. If it doesn't help you to feel a little bit better, make your own picture. Maybe you want it to look more like your mom, or more like how you want your mom to look and feel. Take your time and then draw it for her and for you. Choose a special time to share the picture with your mom.

You can use this picture to help you if you want.

This space is for your Healthy Mom drawing

3. Who else would you like to share the picture with?

    I will share this picture with

Think about what you will say when you share the picture with others.

I will say --

when I share the picture.

Attitude of Gratitude

When one of the people you love the most is feeling really sick it is just natural to feel terrible for them and with them. And sometimes it is hard to think about anything else. You are worried about them; you might feel helpless because all the things you used to do before to make them feel better don't work anymore.

And then there is your life. You still have to go to school. If you have other brothers and/or sisters, and another parent, you might feel torn because you want to still be loving to them. In fact, you might feel like you want to try even harder to show love and affection to your other family members when your mom is so ill.

One step you can take to rise above the sad feelings that darken your once happy home is to think about the things for which you are thankful. At first this may seem really, really hard! That is totally understandable – the rock of your world has been shaken, and you may feel like you are barely hanging on to any feelings at all.

Starting with a small list, 5 things a day, is a good beginning. It helps to write them down in the morning. Starting your day by writing them down helps you to remember them throughout the day. (But if you can't find time in the morning, any time of the day will work.)

You may not be able to think of any at first. Take a few moments alone and relax. Take some deep breaths and close your eyes. Then open them and ask yourself what gives you even a bit of happiness at this moment. It could be

- the sunshine,

- your dog's crazy antics,

- your sister's smile,

- finishing all of your homework last night.

When you have them written down, share them with another family member. Or you might share them with your best friend, a grandparent, or a favorite neighbor. Sharing these lists with your mom can make her feel good, too. This can be something your family does each day to help all of you know that there are some things in your world that are still going well and bring you happiness.

Your attitude of gratitude is a perfect prayer, too. It is a way to thank God for your life just as it is right now.

As we remember the things and people we love, our lists grow and grow. We remember there are parts of our world that make us feel good, and the better you feel the more you can share that good feeling with your sick mom.

Your mom will love knowing you are trying to feel good and that will help her feel good.

Making a gratitude list

1. What about your life still makes you happy? What person, place or thing brings a smile to your face or makes you feel special?

    This person makes me feel so good

    This place helps me to feel good

    This thing makes me feel happy

2. Make a list. Don't worry if day after day you say the same things. It is good to know there are parts of your life that continue to make you feel thankful. Think about when you will share your list with your mom.

    What time is best to share my gratitude list?

3. What other people in your family do you want to share your list with?

4.   This is a list of people, places and things I am thankful for:

I am thankful for   because

I am thankful for   because

I am thankful for   because

I am thankful for   because

I am thankful for   because

5.   Find one person for whom you are grateful and give them a big hug and tell them why.

I am grateful for   , and am going to give them a big hug.

A Book of Your Own

Many days you may feel like there is no one who REALLY understands how you feel. But your feelings are real and important. Describing your feelings on paper can help you express them and give you a way to work through them.

Keeping a diary or journal to record how you are doing day to day is a good way to record your hopes and dreams, your anger and frustrations, your sadness. It is a safe place to voice what may be buried deep down inside of you.

Sometimes writing your feelings and thoughts about your life, your day, your family and friends makes you feel more at peace. Often words are not enough and drawing a picture of your feelings helps you express what your heart feels.

The journal becomes your daily special friend – the one holding your deepest secrets, the one you can pour your heart out to without any danger of being judged. I like to think of it as a way to help your mind and your heart to rise above some of the sadness that can be around you. It also is the perfect place to put your gratitude lists.

It is good to find a special place to spend time with your special book. It might be

- in your room,

- in a corner of the house when no one is around, or

- outside under a tree.

Use a pen, a pencil, crayons, markers – paints, whatever will help you to express how you feel.

Any notebook will work, sometimes lined paper is good, sometimes it might feel better to have blank pages so you can write and draw as big and as free as you want.

Remember, this journal is your personal friend. You can keep it in a safe place that only you know about so you can go to it and share whatever you feel like sharing, whenever you feel like sharing. Sometimes it could be sad or scary feelings and sometimes you will be happy and thankful. Your journal is a place to feel safe expressing it all. Let your feelings tumble right onto the paper. It will help you to feel better.

When my mom
feels better
I want to...

And there may be some days when showing your mom what you wrote or drew will make her feel better or help her to better understand you and how you feel. This book can be a good place to make a list of things you would like to do with your mom when she feels better. That list could include:

- Go to the park,

- Take a walk or a drive,

- Sing my favorite song, or

- Watch our favorite television show together.

Use your diary in whatever way helps you to feel good from day-to-day. Knowing you have this kind of way to show your true feelings will help your mom more than you could guess.

How to start making your own book

1. Choose what kind of notebook or paper you are going to use.

2. Decide if there is a special pen or marker, or set of crayons you want to use.

3. Most importantly, how are you feeling right now? Think about how you can express that feeling the best. Will writing help you get the feelings out or does drawing how you feel seem the best way to get them out?

    I am feeling

    I was feeling

    I want to feel

4. Find a special time each day, if you can, to spend time putting your feelings and what happened to you in your journal. It is your story and what you think and feel is important. What time of day works for you?

5. This book can also be a place to write or draw the things or events you are looking forward to.

I am looking forward to

I am looking forward to

I am looking forward to

6. Your diary can also be a place to write about how your mom seems to be feeling. Sometimes sharing with her about how you feel can be good thing for both of you.

Choose a good time to share these feelings. A good time to share could be at dinner some evenings.

What time works best for you and your family?

It's Okay to Be Angry

Adults often say "life is not fair". Having a very sick mom at your age is truly not fair. Your mom is the one who always takes care of you when you are sick. Your mom is the person in your life who is always strong and smiling when you need her to be. She is the one you go to for a hug and a kiss when you need them.

Now it may seem like she has very little energy for that kind of love, that kind of strength and that feels all wrong. Wishing your life could be back like it was before your mom got sick is very normal.

It does not feel good to watch someone you love so much, and who was the really strong person in your life, feel bad and look weak. Sometimes that can make you feel really frustrated and angry, asking yourself "why is this happening to me and my mom?"

The hard part is we do not have the answers for why this is happening, but we do know for sure that it is okay to be angry, frustrated and sad about what is happening to your mom, and to you.

It is good to let yourself feel mad, so mad you just want to punch something. What you need to figure out is how to recognize your anger and let it out. Letting our feelings out can make us feel so much better because feelings are ways for our very deepest longings, our deepest hurts to be heard. And if they are not heard, that denies a very important part of who we are.

There are good and safe ways to allow your feelings to be heard. Sometimes when you are very angry it helps to run as hard as you can for as long as you can or to sing as loud as you can or to pray with all of your might. Sometimes it helps just to hit your bed mattress with your fist or a belt – saying whatever you really feel in the deepest places in your heart.

If you can find a place where you are by yourself, maybe in the shower or outside in a big field, it can help to yell as loud as you can and scream whatever you feel like telling God or the world.

FEAR

blue

SCARED

Panic

ANGRY!!!

Confused

Pain

MAD!!!

Lonely

SAD.

33

Expressing your true feelings about your mom and yourself and your other family members, about what you are experiencing right now, in loud screams can help. Cry while you scream, let whatever hurts deep down inside you come out loud and clear. There may be some feelings deep down that even make you feel sick to your stomach, or cause you to not be able to sleep at night. Yelling at the way your mom's illness has rocked your world is a way to release feelings that can be very bad for you to keep bottled up inside.

Just like yelling really loud for your team at a sports event can make you feel really good, yelling about how you hate what is happening in this moment can help you feel better, too.

Drawing or painting your feelings with any colors you choose to show how you feel is good. Your journal is great place to keep these pictures so you have a record of how you have been feeling. It is a way to say it is okay, and "I am going to show right here on this piece of paper how I really feel, I don't care what anyone else thinks."

Allowing yourself to be really angry and letting the anger out so no one else gets hurt is healthy. And taking care of you, is good for your mom, too. She needs you to be healthy in your mind and heart. It will help her to feel better, even if it may not seem so on some days.

And guess what else? It is okay to feel really happy even when it seems you should always be sad. Your life is a very rich, wonderful experience and there will be people, places and things that will make you feel wonderful many days. Your happiness will help your mom and other people in your family feel good.

It's okay to feel sad, sorry and angry

1. What are you feeling right now?

   I am feeling

2. Do you have someone you can share these feelings with?

3. If not, what ways can you think of to let your feelings out?

   I could

   I could

   I could

4. Can you find a good time to share how you feel with your mom? She cares and she wants to know.

This is a Beginning

When you first found out your mom was really sick you probably thought and surely felt like your world was ending. Any time something bad happens in our lives, our emotions kick in and can color our view of the world in a very dark way.

It is important to remember that life is full of lessons; each and every thing that happens to us is a way to learn. Yes, it is really hard right now to see your mom going through this illness. But this time in your life can also be a way to learn new things about yourself. It offers you the chance to learn new ways to cope and these are lessons that last a lifetime.

You can use the tools this book has offered as a start. But, you will probably come up with other ways that are helping you to feel better about what is happening around you.

This can be a beginning for you and your family. You can learn new ways of loving yourselves and each other. That can be a silver lining on this dark cloud hanging over your life right now.

Be brave, be tender, and believe you can help your family continue to love each other no matter what happens. You can make a difference in your mom's life and the life of others.

I wish you love and light – and health for you and your mom.

"Gwen wrote a wonderful book and workbook. It will be tremendously helpful for all kids who have a mom who isn't healthy..... whether it's a terminal illness or one who has a cold."

Joan Kelly, CEO, RoarHealth

Healthy Mom Healthy Me is an easy-to-use workbook to help children whose mom is experiencing a serious illness. Children will learn to:

- Recognize and reflect on their feelings.

- Express those feelings constructively.

- Visualize a good outcome for their mom's health.

- Create a journal that can be a safe place to describe what is important to them.

- Understand the value of being grateful every day.

Gwen Ratermann worked in health policy, was a speechwriter and wrote for a small town newspaper. The techniques she describes in *Healthy Mom Healthy Me* helped her family while her husband fought cancer. Since then she has shared these tools with countless others.

Gwen and her husband, Martin, live on the bluffs of the Missouri River.
Visit her at gwenratermann.com.

Wendy Leach is an illustrator from Prairie Village, Kansas. She lives with three wonderful guys, a big one, a little one, and a fuzzy one.

Lightning Source UK Ltd.
Milton Keynes UK
UKHW051336180319

339365UK00006B/67/P